This edition published by Parragon Books
Unit 13–17, Avonbridge Trading Estate, Atlantic Road, Avonmouth, Bristol, BS11 9QD

© 1994 Twin Books Limited

Produced by Twin Books Limited
Kimbolton House, 117a Fulham Road, London, SW3 6RL, England

Directed by CND- Muriel Nathan-Deiller
Illustrated by Van Gool-Lefèvre-Loiseaux

ISBN 0 75250 090 2

Printed and bound in Italy

Thumbelina

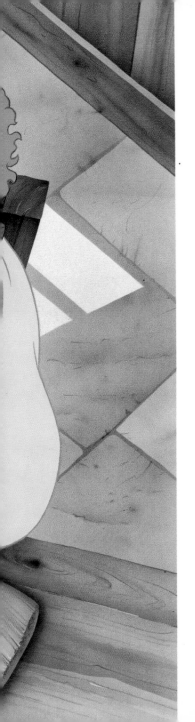

Once upon a time there was a woman who was sad because she had no children. She went to see a witch who lived deep in the nearby woods and said, "Please help me. I would like so much to have a little girl to take care of." In exchange for a few coins the witch gave her a small seed. As soon as the woman got home she planted it in a pot. Then she went to bed and prayed that her wish would be granted.

7

What a surprise she had the next morning. She
ran to the pot and discovered that a magnificent
tulip had grown overnight. The woman was
disappointed that there was no little girl, but the
flower was so beautiful that she gently kissed it.
As her lips touched the petals they opened,
revealing a perfect little girl inside! She was fair
and delicate, and no bigger than the woman's
thumb.

"What can I call you? I know, you're so tiny
I'll call you Thumbelina," the woman said.

That evening she put Thumbelina to bed in a walnut shell, giving her a rose petal as a blanket and a butterfly's wing as a pillow. Thumbelina slept soundly in her new bed, dreaming wonderful dreams.

The next day the woman made Thumbelina a boat to play in by floating a leaf in a plate of water. Thumbelina was so happy as she splashed around that she began to sing. The woman had never heard such a beautiful voice! The happier Thumbelina became, the louder she sang and her lovely, pure voice could be heard throughout the surrounding countryside.

Unfortunately a toad who lived in the pond near the woman's cottage heard Thumbelina singing and thought,

"That girl sings so beautifully, she must be very pretty." In the dead of night, the toad waited until the woman had gone to sleep and hopped through the window and kidnapped Thumbelina as she slept in her bed.

"I've found a wife for my son," he croaked happily as he carried the beautiful girl away, hopping on his large webbed feet over the lily pads.

12

He hopped off to the marsh where his ugly son was waiting.

"What do you think?" he asked, pointing to the sleeping girl. "She's sweet, isn't she?"

"Yes, very pretty," agreed the son. "She will make a delightful wife. But if she sees me, she'll run away!"

"Then let's make sure she can't get away," said the father. He put Thumbelina's cradle on a waterlily leaf in the little stream which crossed the marsh, pushing it far out into the middle.

When Thumbelina woke up the next morning she nearly fell into the water as she climbed out of bed. She was very frightened. She looked and saw the toad and his ugly son watching her from the bank.

"Where am I?" she cried.

"You're with us now," croaked Father Toad, "and you're most welcome."

"But I don't know you!" said Thumbelina. "I want my mother! I want to go home, please take me home, Mr. Toad."

"This is your home from now on," replied the toad. "And this is your future husband." He pointed to his son, the ugly toad!

"The wedding will be tomorrow," said the toad. "There's no time to lose. We must go and get ready for the ceremony. My son will have a new jacket with golden buttons and you shall have a gossamer dress made from dragonfly wings." The toads hopped away smiling.

Poor Thumbelina, who couldn't escape without falling into the water, was so upset that she burst into tears.

19

It happened that some fish in the stream had heard all this. They rushed to help Thumbelina. Really, they thought, such a beautiful creature couldn't marry that awful toad! *Snap!* They bit quickly through the stalk that held the waterlily, so that the leaf floated downstream. They pushed the leaf along with their noses until they grew tired, but Thumbelina was safe.

"Oh, thank you!" cried Thumbelina, as she waved goodbye to the kind fish.

Away went Thumbelina, carried along by the stream far beyond where the toads could reach her. Some birds watched the little girl gliding along the water and chirped happily, "What a delightful little person! How nice she looks! How perfect! How sweet she is!" They would have liked to stop her to have a closer look, but a maybug got there first! Gliding down he landed on the lily pad by Thumbelina's side, caught gently hold of her and carried her up into a tree for safety.

23

The maybug led Thumbelina along a branch. "Don't be afraid," he said. "I just want to introduce you to my family." But when the young lady maybugs saw Thumbelina, they hissed like jealous cats.

"Look," they said, "she has only two legs! She's got no wings at all! Goodness, isn't she ugly!" The maybug had thought Thumbelina was beautiful, but he began to believe the others when they said she was ugly. He picked Thumbelina up and flew down from the tree.

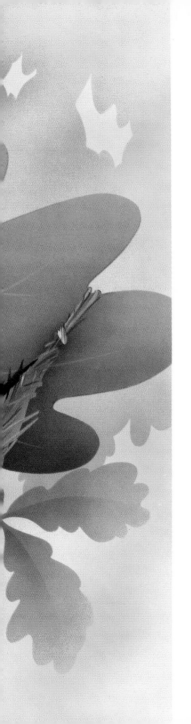

As soon as Thumbelina was alone she made a hammock out of little pieces of straw and sewed them together with spider's web. She chose a leaf to be her sunshade and fixed the hammock under it. It was a lovely house! She was thirsty and hungry, so she sipped a drop of dew and sucked the nectar from a flower. Then she felt better. She still missed her walnut shell cradle, but she was happy in her hammock.

Thumbelina liked living in the forest. She had rainwater to drink, berries to eat, the birds for company and the sun to keep her warm.

Sadly, one day, things began to change. The birds flew away, the leaf which sheltered her withered and fell off the tree and a cold wind blew. Autumn had arrived.

Suddenly everything had changed. There was no sweet grass to lie on, no joyful birdsong in the branches, and nothing left to eat. But it was even worse when winter arrived, bringing snow and frosts.

Thumbelina was cold and unhappy.

Thumbelina decided she must leave the forest. She had no shoes and her feet were freezing, but she walked miles through cornfields, tearing her clothes on the stubble. Finally she found a tiny house with tiny doors and windows and a tiny chimney with smoke billowing out. There must be a fire inside! Cold and hungry she knocked on the door to ask for something to eat. A field mouse opened the door and when he saw her shivering with cold, he kindly invited her in.

31

How nice it was there! The fire burnt brightly and sent a cosy glow around the tiny room. The mouse brought her warm milk to drink and cheese to eat. But he was not alone.

"May I introduce my neighbour, the mole?" he said. Then in a low voice he added, "He's blind, but he's rich! He'd be an excellent husband for you."

"Why do they all want to marry me off?" wondered Thumbelina. But she shook the neighbour's fat hand. She did not wish to appear rude when the mouse had been so kind.

"Would you do me the honour of having a drink at my house?" the mole asked most gallantly. Thumbelina politely accepted. As they all walked along an underground tunnel, she bumped into a bird which lay absolutely still.

"He's sick," she cried.

"Or dead," said the mole. "Those brainless birds sing all summer long and then when winter comes they've nothing to eat. It's the same every year. Don't both trying to help him, they don't help themselves. They play all summer and save nothing for winter. Come along, do!"

Thumbelina reluctantly followed her companions to the mole's house. But that evening, when the others were asleep, she thought about the beautiful songbirds who had cheered her all summer with their songs. She wove a blanket of hay, and crept down the dark underground tunnel to the bird. It was a beautiful swallow. Covering him with the blanket, she hugged him gently to try to warm him.

"His heart is beating!" she whispered. "I knew it! He's just numb with cold!"

The next day she went to see the bird again. She crept quietly along the tunnel. He was awake but very weak. She explained how she'd found and covered him.

"What happened to you?" she asked.

"I got lost," he said. "All my friends flew off to the warm countries. Without you I'd have died of cold and hunger."

"I'll bring you some food every night," said Thumbelina, "and gradually you'll get better. One day you'll be strong enough to fly away. But not before spring!"

Thumbelina was right. She crept back along the tunnel every night and when spring arrived the bird was better. He decided to go and find his friends.

"Come with me," he said to the girl. "You can't spend your whole life underground! I'll carry you on my back up above the clouds and show you some wonderful places!"

"I'd love to," she said, "but the mouse who saved my life would be terribly unhappy. Farewell, little bird. Have a lovely journey off to the sunny countries."

When summer came Thumbelina was very unhappy. She found it difficult to stay shut away in the dark, damp house buried deep underground. She never felt the warmth of the sun or heard the wind blowing in the trees. She sat spinning wool and day dreaming of travelling to sunny places instead of thinking of marrying the tiresome mole.

But the mouse had grown very fond of Thumbelina and didn't want her to go away. He always said, "Hurry, your wedding day is getting close. If you don't hurry up your trousseau will never be finished."

On the wedding day itself, the mole arrived in his bridegroom's suit.

"I've come for my fiancee," he said. Thumbelina ran along the tunnel to take a last look out of the door. She looked up with tears in her eyes. "Goodbye, sun!" she whispered sadly, 'I'll never see you again. Goodbye blue sky, goodbye!"

But as she turned to come in, her friend the swallow suddenly flew down from the sky, his beautiful wings gleaming in the rays of the sun.

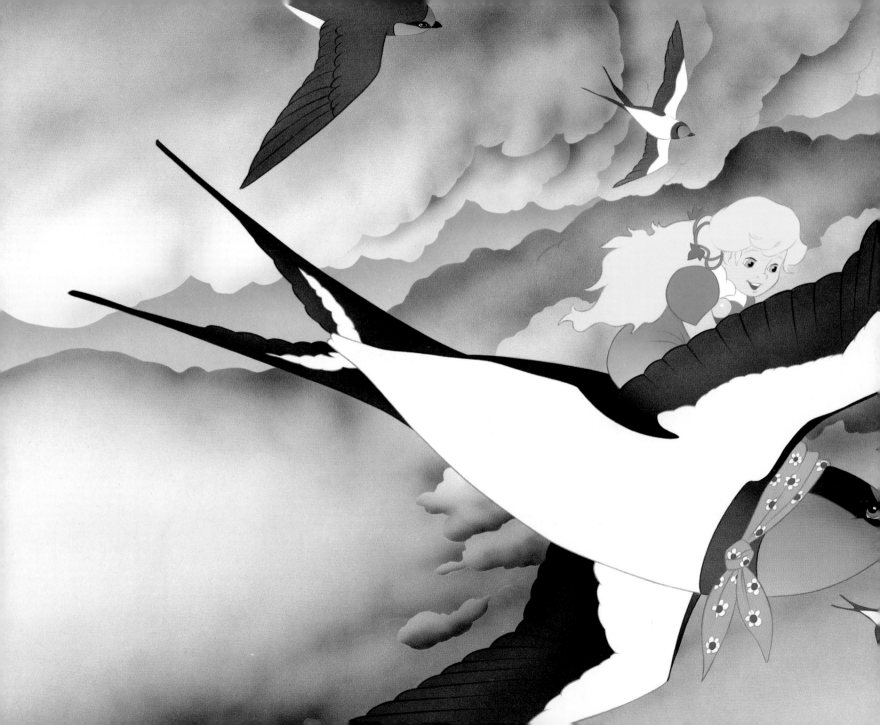

"I came to see how you are getting on," he said kindly.

"I am very unhappy," sighed Thumbelina. "I'm getting married today and after tonight I shall be shut up inside forever."

"That's cruel!" cried the bird. "I beg you to come away with me!" This time the temptation was too strong.

"I'm sorry, little mouse," Thumbelina murmured. Then she ran to the bird and jumped on to his back.

Once again it was autumn. This time the bird was determined to fly far enough away to find a sunny country where there is no winter. What a wonderful journey they had!

They flew over mountains and across the sea and came to an enchanting country full of golden grapes, sweet-scented lemons and meadows of wild flowers. The bird, tired but happy, landed near a magnificent palace on a hillside. It was surrounded by tall trees and gardens full of brilliantly coloured flowers.

Thumbelina looked around her. There were so many beautiful things to see and birds singing in every tree.

"Choose your favourite flower," said the bird. "It will be your home." Thumbelina stepped down and walked from one flower to another. It was very hard to choose, but finally she decided.

"This one," she said. Then she got a surprise. There was already someone living on it. "Oh, I beg your pardon!" said Thumbelina.

The young man on the flower looked at her and smiled.

"Hello!" he called. He was no bigger than Thumbelina. He had beautiful eyes and a splendid gold crown on his head. Thumbelina thought he was very handsome. Suddenly she gasped in wonder, for she saw that there were also two transparent wings fluttering on his back. "Who are you?" asked Thumbelina. "You have wings. Are you a bird, or a maybug?"

"No, I'm the King of the Flowers," he chuckled. "And you?"

"Thumbelina is my name." The King thought she was the loveliest maiden he'd ever seen. He put his crown on her head, then leaned towards her and gently took her hand. "Will you be my Queen?" he asked.

Thumbelina thought how different he was from the hideous toad and the blind old mole, and said, "Yes."

The King kissed her.

Thumbelina was so happy she began to sing
again. As she sang, every beautiful flower began
to open and from each one came a fairy. They
all had tiny wings and fluttered around
Thumbelina, who clapped her hands with
delight. "They're the princes and princesses of
my kingdom," said the King. "They've come to
bring us wedding presents."

Thumbelina was given all kinds of delightful gifts: a new dress, soft slippers, perfume from the flowers and honey from the bees, but her favourite was a pair of delicate wings. They were fastened to Thumbelina's back.

"From now on you'll be able to fly like me," said the King. And together they flew off above the flowers. They flew as high as the birds, looking down on to their kingdom below.

And that is how Thumbelina became Queen of the Flowers. She wanted to say thank you to her friend the bird who'd saved her from a life without sunshine and song, but he had already gone. He travelled the world, stopping to tell his story wherever he found people with true loving hearts who would listen to the tale and understand it.